𝒜s a reporter, editor, business writer, and marketing communications consultant, F.I. Goldhaber produced news stories, feature articles, essays, editorial columns, and reviews for newspapers, corporations, governments, and non-profits in five states. Now, her poems, short stories, novelettes, essays, and reviews appear in paper, electronic, and audio magazines, ezines, newspapers, calendars, and anthologies. She published five erotica novels and a novella under another name.

In addition to paper, electronic, and audio publications, F.I. shares her words at events in Portland, Seattle, Salem, Keizer and on the radio. She appeared at venues such as Wordstock, Oregon Literary Review, PDX SynesthiA, bookstores, libraries, and community colleges; gives presentations on subjects as diverse as marketing, writing erotica, and building volunteer organizations; and taught Introduction to Indie Publishing at Portland Community College and as a weekend intensive.

http://goldhaber.net/

The Lover and The Patient

Which would you pick? ... Raymond must choose between the only man he ever loved and his career.

Dimensions

Caught between worlds, Lora struggles to survive. ... Lost in another dimension, one of her own creation, Lora must endure until her wife finds a way to repair the door that separates them.

Queer Notion

Must society's bias separate two young lovers? ... Arrested for violating gender laws, Louie and Ryan must promise never to see each other again to avoid ten years in detention. Desperate, Louie researches the laws' history and learns of another option.

Originally
published in
Queer Shorts

The Lover

and

The Patient

Which would you choose?

Three Stories

F.I. Goldhaber

The Lover and The Patient: Three Short Stories

Fantastic Worlds Publishing

ISBN: 978-1-937839-25-3

The Lover and The Patient first published by Merge Press in *Queer Shorts*, 2006

Fantastic Worlds Publishing
http://fantasticworldspublishing.com
P.O. Box 80766
Portland OR 97280

Table of Contents

Acknowledgements

Many thanks to all those I have learned from through the years, especially the Wordos professional writers workshop and Larry Brooks. Thanks also to those who have freely shared their knowledge online, notably Dean Wesley Smith and Kristine Kathryn Rusch. Those who inspired me to pursue writing from an early age include Ruth Wright, my fifth and sixth grade teacher at Randolph Elementary School in Huntsville, Alabama; Nancy Travis, my freshman English teacher at Clear Creek High School in Texas; and most prominently my parents, Jerry and Bev Goldhaber. Very special thanks to my editor, Laurie Lawhon of Fine Tune Your Words, and my beloved husband Joel Goldhaber.

The Lover

and

The Patient

Which would you choose?

**Originally published
in *Queer Shorts***

F.I. Goldhaber

The Lover and The Patient

By F.I. Goldhaber

Raymond stuffed his hat and gloves in his coat pocket, hung his coat on the wall hook, and dropped into the black fake-leather booth in the back of the half-empty restaurant. Elbows on the plastic sheet covering the tablecloth, head in his hands, he tried to distance himself from the pathos at the AIDS clinic without thinking about the empty apartment waiting for him down the street.

He opened his eyes and looked up to see a busty woman with straightened hair holding an order pad and a pencil.

"You look like you could use a drink. Dewar's, right?"

Raymond nodded.

"You want something to eat with that? We have a real nice Blue Plate Special. It includes meatloaf, mashed potatoes with gravy, and green beans for just $10.95."

"Sure," Raymond said, glad to have the decision made for him. For the past three years, Jonathan had done all the cooking. Until his lover's abrupt, unexplained departure two weeks ago, Raymond never had to think about what to eat for dinner.

The January wind whistled through the restaurant, and Raymond looked up to see Jonathan walking through the front door. For a moment Raymond's heart beat faster, and he wished he had taken time to change out of his scrubs and take a shower. A skinny, pale blond in a passé black shirt and tie followed Jonathan to a table near the front of the restaurant. To Raymond's dismay, the two didn't take chairs across from each other, but sat with just the corner separating them. The man accompanying Jonathan looked vaguely familiar, but Raymond couldn't place him. Jonathan's unruly red hair, kissable freckled face, and long lanky form tore at the wounds in Raymond's heart. He should have arrived home from the clinic to find Jonathan putting some finishing touches on his Spaghetti Carbonara or Veal Marsala. Later, Jonathan would have rubbed Raymond's shoulders to help him relax after his horrid day.

The server set Raymond's drink in front of him. He lifted the glass, intending to take just a sip of the whiskey, but finished it instead.

"Another?" The server raised one eyebrow. She glanced at Jonathan, then back at Raymond, and answered her own question. "I'll be right back."

Raymond stared at the table where Jonathan sat. Although he could only see the back of Jonathan's head, Raymond had an unobstructed view of the man with him. He blinked to clear the tears from his eyes, trying to remember where he had seen this man before.

The server returned with another drink, set it on the table, and sat down across from Raymond. "Look, I know it's none of my business, but, obviously, he's moved on, and you need to also."

Raymond stared at the woman and realized she had waited on him and Jonathan countless times in the past. He should have known better than to eat somewhere they had frequented together, but Raymond just couldn't face another night of takeout in an apartment that echoed with memories, and was too tired to venture into an unfamiliar restaurant.

"I'm Jackie," the server reached a hand across the table. "You're Raymond, right?"

Raymond nodded and shook Jackie's hand.

"People don't realize how much a server can pick up on relationships. Especially relationships of regulars. I assume the fact that you're alone and he's dating again means that he broke up with you?"

Again Raymond nodded, and his gaze drifted back to Jonathan and his companion.

"Raymond, honey, you're a looker. You've got amazing blue eyes, and I bet your hair's softer than silk. And even hidden in those oversized scrubs, I can tell you've got a very nice build." Raymond gave Jackie a long look. "I'm sure you could find a dozen interested guys tomorrow, if you wanted to."

Raymond couldn't keep his eyes off of Jonathan and his date. A flash of recognition punched him in the stomach. The man dating his former lover was a patient from the clinic. Closing his eyes, Raymond visualized his record: Dan Smith — probably not his real name — HIV positive.

"Why did he break up with you?"

Raymond opened his eyes, grabbed his drink, and downed it in one swallow. He looked at Jackie.

"You okay?"

"Not really. I don't know why Jonathan left." No amount of tearful pleading, while Jonathan packed boxes and suitcases, had elicited an explanation. "Just a few months ago, we were talking about going up to Canada and getting married."

"But?"

"Jonathan always wanted a big wedding: all our friends, people we worked with, our families."

"And you?"

"I would've settled for registering as domestic partners at the Municipal Building and maybe a small celebration with just a few close friends. I try to stay low-key. I mean, I didn't hide our relationship or anything, but I didn't flaunt it either. And my family's all in Idaho. Most of them don't know I'm gay; not that it matters. I don't have much to do with them beyond Christmas visits." Raymond had only come out to his sister Sara. When he did, her suggestion that he move out of state to do his residency convinced him not to come out to anyone else.

"Honey, did you ever think that maybe your lover left because he got tired of being in the closet with you?"

"But I'm not..."

"I'd better run before the boss catches me socializing. But I get off at nine. If you need someone to talk to, we could go for coffee."

Jackie stood up and took Raymond's empty glass. "Refill?"

"Yeah."

Raymond studied the back of Jonathan's head in disbelief. *Did he leave because I wouldn't take him home to spend Christmas with my Fundamentalist redneck family who would treat us both as pariahs?* By the time Raymond returned from his annual Idaho pilgrimage, he had forgotten about the fuss Jonathan made when he again bought only one ticket to Boise. Raymond had attributed Jonathan's preoccupation on New Year's Eve to a falling out Jonathan had with Herb and Clive, the hosts of the party they attended. He wondered now what really caused Jonathan's reticence that night.

Now Jonathan, the only man Raymond ever truly loved, was dating someone with HIV. Raymond wondered if they had slept together yet. He could remember the smell of Jonathan's skin, the caress of his hands, the heat of the passion they shared. Raymond had never known a lover as wonderful as Jonathan, and he cringed to think of him with another man. Maybe Jackie was right. Raymond thought about the fundraisers for the clinic he had attended alone, and the Medical Society social events he always skipped instead of attending by himself or with Jonathan. Raymond wiped away a tear with his napkin.

"You can't commit to anything," Jonathan had shouted at him two months ago after Raymond told a Gay Men's Health Crisis representative he would have to get back to him about purchasing tickets to a dance-a-thon. "You can't even commit to being gay." Raymond didn't see the connection. And in a country that considered preventing same-sex marriage more important than stopping an unjustifiable war, he didn't think it safe to parade around advocating gay rights.

Raymond watched Dan run the back of one finger down Jonathan's jaw, pausing at the corner of his mouth, and fumed. He knew Jonathan wouldn't date Dan if he were aware of his HIV status. Raymond started to pull himself from the booth, but hesitated. If he told Jonathan that Dan had HIV, he risked losing his medical license. If he couldn't practice medicine, he'd probably end up destitute, and back in Idaho.

Dan touched Jonathan's arm, stood up, and headed toward the back of the restaurant. He walked past Raymond's table, almost knocking over Jackie, who had a plate of food in one hand and a glass of whiskey in the other, and into the men's room. Raymond hesitated, then rose from the booth and followed him.

"Honey, don't do anything foolish," Jackie whispered.

Raymond ignored her. He just wanted to *talk* to Dan. In the restroom, the single stall was empty and Dan stood alone at the urinal.

"Have you told him you're positive?"

Dan turned, sending his stream against the stall wall. He glared at Raymond and turned back. "That's none of your business, Doc."

"Actually, it is my business. It's a public health issue. As a clinic director, I have an obligation to make sure my patients behave responsibly and don't spread the virus." He shook his head. This wasn't just a clinic patient. This man was seducing someone Raymond loved.

"Don't worry, Doc. I'll wear a condom."

"Including when you're in his mouth?" When they first started seeing each other, Jonathan's reluctance to use condoms, despite his concerns about contracting HIV, had appalled Raymond.

Dan zipped up his pants. "Don't say a fucking word, Doc. I can get your license revoked."

"You're endangering someone else's health without informing him of the risk he's facing. The law says I'm not supposed to let you do that."

Dan stuck his hands under the faucet for a few seconds, grabbed a paper towel, and headed for the door. Raymond blocked his exit.

"You interfere and I'll bring charges." Dan poked at Raymond's chest.

Raymond stepped aside and Dan stormed out. Head down, Raymond trudged back to his table and sat down in front of a steaming plate of food he couldn't eat. He watched Dan and Jonathan hold hands, their fingers laced together. *I should tell him. But Jonathan has some obligation to protect his own health, doesn't he? And if I do tell Jonathan and Dan makes a public stink, word would spread in the community and others would avoid testing for fear of getting outed.* A story like that could make national news. With a hometown boy involved, the *Idaho Statesman* would surely pick it up.

With thumb and forefinger, Raymond massaged the bridge of his nose. What if Jonathan had asked about Dan's status and Dan lied to him?

Raymond finished his drink, picked up his fork, and pushed his food around his plate. He scooped crumbled meatloaf mixed with mashed potatoes into his mouth, and forced himself to chew and swallow. Jackie reappeared.

"You like?"

He nodded, even though he hadn't tasted anything.

She reached for his empty glass. "One more?"

He nodded again.

"You aren't driving, are you?"

Raymond shook his head. He managed to force down another mouthful before she returned. He picked up his glass, but just swirled it around. Another drink would push him past tipsy to inebriated. In college, he always acted foolishly after his third drink: he'd go home with strangers or suck them off in men's rooms. Since graduation, he usually limited himself to two drinks. Now he needed to think clearly, and regretted his last drink. He didn't need another.

He still loved Jonathan, despite his anger over his abrupt departure. Raymond missed their Sunday walks in Central Park, the nights they spent dancing at the Ember's Club, the Mets games they attended in the summer, their weekend trips to Poughkeepsie. After everything they had shared, the thought of Jonathan as a patient at the clinic made Raymond's stomach churn and his head ache. He pushed his plate away and toyed with his glass again. Maybe if Raymond promised to be more out, to take him to Boise next Christmas, Jonathan would come back.

Raymond leaned his chin on his hand. "Commitment phobic," Jonathan had called him. "The only decision you ever make is to avoid making a decision." Raymond *had* let Jonathan make most of the choices in their relationship. Jonathan always asked him out and chose where they would go. And after six months together, it was Jonathan who decided he would move into Raymond's apartment rather than pay rent for one he rarely used. Raymond tried to remember the last time he told Jonathan he loved him without hearing the words from Jonathan first.

He watched Jonathan and Dan finish their dinner, put on their coats, and head for the door. Jonathan draped one arm over Dan's shoulders, and Dan wrapped an arm around Jonathan's waist. *This time*, Raymond thought. He stood, dropped two twenties on the table, tilted his head back, and poured more Scotch down his throat. Slamming the glass down on the table, he shuddered, grabbed his coat, and walked after them.

When he reached the door, he paused and shook his head in a vain attempt to clear the alcohol fog. He stared at the door handle, trying to remember what he'd planned to do. He realized that he had, for once, made a decision about his personal life without consulting anyone else.

He jerked the door open and embraced the winter cold.

𝕽

Dimensions

Caught between worlds,
Lora struggles to survive

F.I. Goldhaber

Dimensions

By F.I. Goldhaber

Lora sat on the deck, sipping her morning brew, and watched hikers wander through her living room. Normally folks didn't trudge up Salal Hill this early on a Thursday. But a few hundred feet below, Cobble Beach already teamed with folks out for the low tide, searching for scarce remnants of marine life.

The hikers stopped in the kitchen to admire the view of Yaquina Head lighthouse. Lora could see their lips moving and wondered what words the panoramic view inspired. Sound didn't cross into her dimension.

"Hon, where's my transit pass, I need to go to the office today," Rakal called from the bedroom.

Lora found her rummaging through her dresser drawers. "Did you look in your wallet?"

"Of course."

Lora lifted Rakal's billfold from her pocket and thumbed through her identicard, credit chip, and snapshots. She found the transit pass stuck between a wedding photo and a picture of them posing with a foot in either dimension while the house was under construction. She paused to admire the firmer torsos and tighter leg muscles from the days when they had to climb hills to reach the view that they now enjoyed from every window of their home.

"Here's your transit pass." She ran her fingers through Rakal's shoulder-length brown hair, just starting to grey at the temples, and kissed her on the forehead.

"I *know* I looked in there." She scrunched her eyebrows together. "Thanks." She took the pass and wallet, giving Lora's hand a quick smooch.

"I'd better get to work myself." Lora smiled. "What time will you be home?"

"Late, probably. Liam's called in everyone within a day's train ride of the Portland office. We'll meet all day and probably have dinner at Ripost." Rakal tousled Lora's short auburn curls with both hands and rubbed her nose against hers. "At least I won't have to stay overnight in the city, and tomorrow we can talk about what you want to do for the holiday."

Lora returned to the living room. The interdimensional port whined and glimmered blue when Rakal went through it into the garage that anchored their home to the earth plane. Settling down in the recliner with her tablet, Lora reminded herself that she needed to retrieve a spare battery when she went through the portal to retrieve lunch from the fridge in the garage.

The Internet connection cut out halfway through her first meeting. Lora hoped it would come back up before her scheduled conference with her boss in Japan. She finished the report she needed for that encounter and got a fair amount of data analysis completed before her stomach growled. Shutting down the tablet, she slipped the battery out and headed for the portal door.

The handle wouldn't turn. She jiggled it, but she couldn't get the brass lever to budge. Lora slipped the battery into her pocket and grabbed the handle with both hands. Even pushing down with all her weight, she couldn't make it move. Sweat made her palms slip off the handle. Her chest tightened and her hands shook. Everything necessary to survive for any length of time in this dimension was on the other side of the portal door: food and water; the electricity to recharge the batteries which operated the lights, the cleaning and toilet equipment; and the replacement battery for her tablet with its Internet connection — her only communication option.

She took a deep breath. *Mustn't panic.* When the Internet connection was restored, she could email for assistance. The worst possibility — if the problem with the portal caused the Internet outage — just meant she would have to wait until Rakal returned from her meeting, found the portal inoperable, and called someone out to repair it. Lora tried to relax the tightness in her chest by mentally inventorying the kitchen. She had a five-gallon bottle of water in addition to whatever remained in the cooler, and a variety of MREs and packaged snack foods in the cupboards. If necessary, should the problem prove difficult to repair, she could get by for a week or more.

She had looked forward to finishing off the pasta left over from their excursion into the city last night. Instead, Lora decided to try one of the new faux chicken MREs for lunch. But when she opened the cupboard, she muttered "What the hell." She knew she had purchased at least a dozen MREs to keep around for emergencies when she shopped last. But she only found three in the cupboard, plus a can of ground caffeine, half a bag of Terra chips, and an unopened package of gingersnaps. Rummaging through the house, Lora discovered a dish full of stale mints on the coffee table in the living room, a half-eaten package of peanut butter wafers in Rakal's desk, and a third of a protein bar on the windowsill next to the exercise bike.

She bit her lip to keep from bursting into tears, gathered her rations on the kitchen counter, and stared at them in dismay. Lifting the bottle from the cooler, she found that barely an inch of water covered the bottom of the ceramic jug. Rakal must have used the last when she brewed the caffeine and, in her rush to get to Portland, had left the empty for Lora to exchange. She sat down at the kitchen table with her head in her hands.

"Mustn't panic." Even if Rakal didn't return home until really late, she could get a technician out first thing in the morning. Lora forced herself to take deep, steady breaths. Still, with the holiday weekend approaching, she should plan for the worst. If the technician had to send for parts, they might not arrive until Tuesday. Safest bet would be to divide her food into six portions, so it would last until Tuesday night.

Doing the math in her head to steady her nerves while she replaced the water bottle, Lora calculated that if she only used the water for drinking, she could allow herself fifty ounces a day, together with half an MRE, an ounce of Terra chips, four gingersnaps, and five mints. She hated peanut butter, but would need the calories from the wafers. The remains of the protein bar would serve as emergency rations.

Deciding to save the half MRE for her evening meal, Lora measured out six ounces of water and placed fourteen Terra chips and two of the ginger snaps on a small plate. Normally she would eat her lunch while reading the news online. Instead she tried to make a formal meal out of her rations. But, despite taking tiny bites and chewing everything thoroughly, lunch only lasted five minutes. Leaving the plate and glass on the table, Lora tried the portal again. It didn't budge. She put the battery back in her tablet, turned it on long enough to determine she still couldn't connect to the Internet, and shut it down.

Thinking a breath of fresh air might help keep the panic at bay, she went back out on the deck. Except for the trio of hikers who had paraded through her living room that morning, no one had climbed up the steep hill that towered above Yaquina Head. A few die-hards trudged through the mounds of polished lava cobblestones on the beach. Tourists stood in line for admittance to the tall white lighthouse, and a couple of lonely auklets swooped through the air above the rocks offshore.

Lora pushed away the panic with memories of the excitement she and Rakal had shared when they got approval to build their house in the alternate dimension, allowing them to enjoy the view of Yaquina Head every day of the year. They had come here to visit the tidepools on their third date, and Rakal had proposed to her a year later on top of the hill, on the very spot where the house now perched.

Lora looked at the salal-covered expanse below the deck. It seemed so close — as if she could climb over the deck railing, hike down the hill, then walk back up the road to the Interpretive Center. There she could ask someone to call Rakal's cell. But, nothing could pass from one dimension to the other without going through a portal. When they first moved in, Rakal had played around, throwing pebbles at the hikers when they walked through the living room. The rocks just passed through the intruders and made marks on the wall.

Her chest tightening again, Lora went inside to check the portal and the Internet connection once more.

By Sunday evening, Lora's tablet would no longer power up. When she couldn't get the handle to budge, she pounded on the portal door. "Stop," she told herself. But she kept hammering with her fists, desperate to force the barrier between her and the earth plane to open.

"Mustn't panic." Lora forced herself to pull her bruised fists from the metal portal door and trudged into the living room. "Mustn't panic." She tried to imagine a scenario that would explain her wife's continued absence, one that didn't include a lengthy disabling of the portal. When Rakal returned to the garage on the small lot they owned in Sherwood Thursday night, she would have called for someone to repair the portal. She probably couldn't have gotten technicians to drive the twenty miles from Portland before Friday. More than likely they had to order parts which wouldn't arrive until Tuesday morning. Surely the technicians would have the portal fixed by the end of that day.

"Hey, Babe, what's up?" Rakal walked through the portal's glimmer. "Sorry I had to work most of the weekend. But we've still got tomorrow if you want to go somewhere."

Lora stared at her. Then her eyes widened. She made a mad dash for the portal door, but it had swung closed and the handle wouldn't move. She collapsed onto the tile floor, sobbing — the panic she fought while waiting for Rakal to get home enveloped her like waves dragging her out to sea. The MRE she had finished half an hour earlier threatened to regurgitate.

"What in the world is wrong with you, Hon?" Rakal knelt down in front of Lora, drawing her into her arms. "Goodness, you've gotten a little ripe. Is the cleanser on the fritz again? Why didn't you email the repair shop?"

Lora tried to answer, but only a sob escaped her lips. *How can she think of bathing at a time like this?* She pointed a shaking finger at the portal. "Broken."

"What in the world are you talking about? I just came through. The portal worked fine." Rakal stood and pulled up on the handle. It didn't move. She pulled down. Nothing. Her face paled and beads of sweat appeared under her bangs. She jumped up and let her weight fall against the handle. Nothing. With her body tensed and her fists clenched, Rakal drew back her foot.

If she puts enough strength into the kick she'll break her leg. Terrified Rakal would hurt herself,

Lora grabbed her foot. Rakal lost her balance and collapsed next to her. She crawled into her arms and they clung to each other. "The Internet's down, too. We can't get help and there's almost no food left." Although Rakal couldn't solve their problems, some of Lora's panic eased when she shared all her worries of the past four days with her wife. "I've tried to conserve, thinking that you found the portal broken when you came back to the garage Thursday night and that you sent for a technician."

"You didn't get my email? Liam decided that as long as he had us all in one place we should work until we finished the project. I've only had about ten hours sleep since I left, and I had to go through the cleanser with my clothes on since I didn't have anything to change into."

Lora shook her head, staring at her in disbelief. "At least you've had plenty of food."

Rakal smiled and her blue eyes brightened. "Liam did send us all home with a gift for our partners to make up for keeping us most of the holiday weekend." She grabbed her haversack and pulled it across the floor. Unzipping it, she extracted a nine-piece box of Moonstruck Chocolate truffles and handed it to Lora.

Clutching the blue and gold box to her chest, Lora stared at the tablet inside the bag. Since Rakal could get through the portal, maybe the Internet had come back up as well. "Do you have battery life?"

"Sure, I just switched the batteries." She

pulled out three more batteries of various sizes. "These were all charged so I brought them in with me, too."

Lora grabbed the smallest one and ran to her tablet. Still holding the truffle box in one hand, she switched the batteries and powered up. No connectivity. She shut it down. Tears seeped out of her eyes. Not knowing what else to do, she ran a thumbnail along the edge of the box to break the seal. Lifting the lid, she took a deep breath and sucked in the aroma of rich cocoa, allowing herself to forget everything else for just a moment. With trembling fingers, she lifted a pear-shaped truffle to her nose and inhaled the intoxicating scent of brandy. She stuck out her tongue, carefully balanced the truffle on the center, and withdrew her tongue into her mouth. Pressing upwards, she released the flavors of pear, brandy, and dark chocolate.

When she finally permitted herself to swallow, she looked up to see Rakal watching her. She, too, had tears in her eyes. "I'm so sorry, Lora."

Lora waited until the last bits of flavor disappeared from her tongue, cascading through her mouth, giving her a moment free from panic. Panic crept back into her chest as the flavors dissipated. "Sorry for what?"

"Working on the project this last couple of weeks, I kept getting midnight munchies. I never felt like going through the portal, so I ate most of the snacks and then started in on the

MREs. I figured I'd pick up some more after we finished the design work. I never imagined you'd get stuck here with nothing to eat."

"Not *nothing*. I rationed it out so it could last until Tuesday. I figured it might take longer to get the portal fixed because of the holiday weekend. But, I've only got one MRE left, some chips, and cookies." She lifted the box. "And now these. Would you like one? They're wonderful."

Rakal shook her head and Lora carefully replaced the lid.

"You can have the rest of the food in the house. I've stuffed my face for the last several days. Liam kept saying we needed to keep our strength up and he brought in meals every few hours."

Lora tried not to imagine. Anyone who would splurge and buy thirty-credit boxes of chocolates for the partners of a dozen employees probably provided his workers with the best takeout available in Portland. Her stomach rumbled.

"At least you can clean up." Rakal held up the largest of the three batteries.

"The cleanser has at least one more cycle before it needs recharging. I was saving it for tomorrow, so I wouldn't stink when you finally got through the portal on Tuesday." She realized that her voice sounded flat and dead. *Beats panicky.*

"You'll feel better if you get cleaned up." Rakal handed her the battery. "Do we have any more caffeine? I'll make you some." She held up the third battery and waved it under her nose. "Bet you could use a cup."

Lora felt the blood drain from her face and the panic return in force. "We only have a hundred and ten ounces of water left." They might survive without food for several weeks, but when the water ran out they wouldn't last three days. Her breath came in gasps.

Rakal frowned. "Okay, no caffeine then. You can still get cleaned up if you want."

Lora couldn't think of a reason not to. Perhaps a cleansing would help her calm down. When she emerged and pulled on a fresh shirt and slacks, she found Rakal in the dining room. She had opened a bottle of Pinot and filled two glasses. Next to one she had placed a plate with six Terra chips surrounding a pyramid-shaped truffle. "Hey, wine is liquid, right. I found two bottles of red and one of white in the rack. We can use that to keep hydrated."

"Don't think it works that way." Lora sat in the chair that Rakal pulled out for her. "But, we may as well enjoy what we have while we can." The flatness had returned.

With a wry smile, Rakal lifted her glass and touched Lora's, making them chime. She almost managed to smile back.

Lora didn't wake Monday morning until almost ten o'clock. Rakal had already left their bed, so she pulled on her robe and went looking for her. She found a note on the kitchen table.

"Lora, darling, I know the two of us can't last long on the water that's left. I'm going to try to climb down from the deck and see if I can figure a way to get from this dimension back to the earth plane. When I do, I'll get you out, I promise. But if I don't succeed, at least you can survive until someone figures out we're missing. Last night was wonderful. Love you forever. Rakal."

Lora ran out onto the deck screaming "Rakal!" A few hikers struggled up the hill, and many people climbed around on Cobble Beach or roamed about the lighthouse grounds. Nowhere could she see any sign of Rakal. Lora couldn't breathe. Should she go after her? But she had no idea if Rakal had successfully climbed down to a solid surface or if she'd plummeted onto the rocks far below and floated lifeless in the sea. If Rakal had found a way to travel in this dimension, Lora had no clue which way she would have walked. She didn't even know how long ago her wife had left. Weeping, Lora crawled back in the bed, seeking Rakal's scent. She curled up into a ball, ranting at Rakal in her mind. *How could you commit suicide?* Even if Lora's chances of survival increased, she didn't believe anyone would rescue her in time. "Why didn't you take me with you?" she wailed. "We should have stayed together."

When hikers walked into the living room, Lora leapt out of bed, charged out of the bedroom, and grabbed for the nearest arm. She couldn't grasp it. "Please, you've got to help me!" They didn't respond. She jumped up and down in front of them and even held open her robe. They walked right through her. Lora fainted.

By cutting back to eating once a day and only drinking twenty ounces of water, Lora managed to make her rations last until Friday. She had stopped expecting a rescue, stopped doing anything except going through the motions of survival. With no hope, she had no reason to panic. That and a glass of wine made it possible to sleep at night. Although she only checked for an Internet connection once in the morning and once at night, both her and Rakal's tablet batteries had died by Thursday evening. Not that it really mattered.

Saturday morning, Lora dragged herself out of bed, although she wondered why. She had finished the wine, drinking the last consumable substance in the house, before she crawled into bed last night. Her eyes no longer produced moisture, so she couldn't cry. The hikers in the living room couldn't help her. She wondered if she could force the portal open with tools. Surely Rakal would have explored that option before climbing off the deck. Still, she supposed she should at least try. She rummaged through the kitchen drawer where they kept assorted hardware used for minor repairs and found several screwdrivers.

Examining the portal handle, Lora couldn't see any way of removing it from inside. She tried to stick one of the screwdrivers under the brass plate at the handle's base, but couldn't pry it off the door. Putting the tip of the largest screwdriver in between the portal door and the frame, she pushed against it, trying to use it to lever the portal door open. Nothing would budge. Lora left the screwdriver sticking out of the narrow gap and wandered out onto the deck.

She stood looking out at the ocean pounding on the rocks hundreds of feet below and wondered what Rakal had found when she climbed down. Water maybe? Berries or nuts? That sounded hopeful. No one had ever found evidence of animal life larger than mollusks in this dimension, but plant life was abundant. Would the plants poison or nourish her? "Does it matter?"

Lora returned to the bedroom and pulled on a pair of cargo pants and a cotton shirt. She filled the pockets in the pants with bug spray, bandages, sunscreen, and other protective gear. A ball cap, waterproof jacket, and hiking boots made her feel as prepared as possible for the world outside her windows.

Before she could frighten herself by thinking about the consequences, Lora straddled the deck railing then swung her other leg over to balance on the outside. She secured one foot between the balusters on the outer rim and let the other hang down. Still no contact with the ground. Clinging to the balusters, she got down on her knees and stuck her foot down further. Nothing. Taking a deep breath, Lora wrapped both hands around the corner support post and hung from the deck, her feet dangling in the air. As her grip gave out and her hands slipped from the balusters, she heard the screwdriver clatter against the tiles and saw the glimmer of the portal door opening.

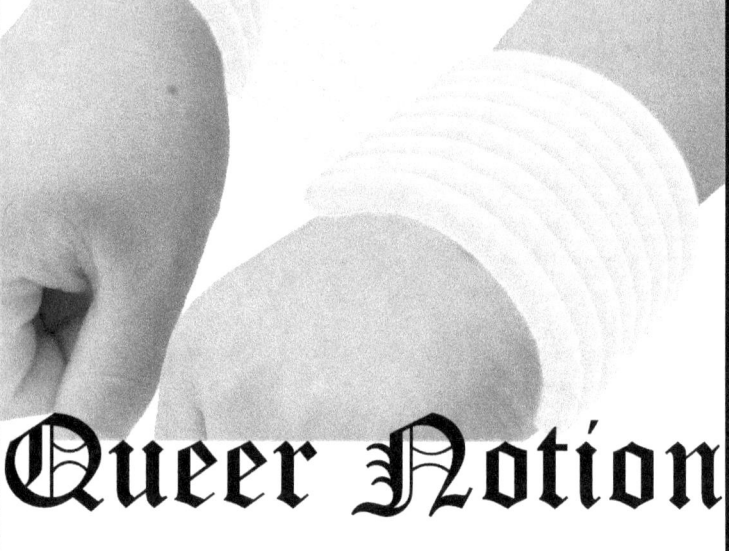

Queer Notion

**Must society's bias
separate two young lovers?**

F.I. Goldhaber

Queer Notion

By F.I. Goldhaber

Louie stroked Ryan's skin, warmed from the rays of the late afternoon sun that poured through the window of the uninhabited dwell. "We've at least gotta tell our parents."

Ryan ran his fingers through Louie's short, red hair. "They'll turn us in."

They kissed. Conversation ceased until, sated, they pulled on their clothes and prepared to make their separate ways home.

"I'd rather they find out from us than the Morality Patrol." Louie checked for skewed clothing in the reflective storage doors. Deceptively innocent bright green eyes gazed back at her from a pale, freckled face. She scowled. "We'll get found out eventually."

"If our parents know and don't report us, they'll get arrested, too." Ryan lifted his long brown hair out from under the collar of his red, sleeveless shirt. Almost two meters of lean, muscular build and an unerring aim had earned him a full spaceball scholarship to Wa-Mass York U. Their relationship would disqualify him and end his pro sports ambitions.

"We just have to make them understand that we're in love." Louie looked up and got lost in Ryan's intense brown eyes.

His dark brows drew together and he shook his head. "No one'll accept falling in love as an excuse for violating gender laws." He opened the dwell door a crack and peeked out into the corridor. After planting a kiss on Louie's lips, he darted outside. Louie paced for the five minutes Ryan needed to ride the lift down eighteen levels and get clear of the structure, waited another five, then exited the dwell.

Three officers in the dark green uniforms of the Morality Patrol stood in front of the lifts, hands on their energy wands. Off to one side, Ryan leaned his shoulder against the wall, his head hanging low, his wrists cuffed behind his back. Dazed, Louie heard one of the Mor-cops say, "You're under arrest for illegal fornication." The woman pulled Louie's arms back and the electrocuffs generated an eerie tingling sensation.

The officers led the lovers out an eighteenth floor exit into a waiting hovercraft. The two men sat in the front and the woman took a seat between Ryan and Louie in back. Louie watched tall structures drift by through a blur of tears.

"Stop sniveling, you little pansy." The officer poked Louie with the handle of the energy wand hanging from the belt on her hip. "Unless you really want something to cry about."

In the rearview mirror, Louie saw Ryan's face contorted in a grimace and wondered if the officer had burned him with her wand. Blinking rapidly to stem the increasing flow of tears, Louie cowered from the officer's glare.

The hovercraft floated next to the platform on the thirty-second floor of an immense structure near the center of the City. The officers jerked Ryan and Louie out of the hovercraft by their upper arms and dragged them inside. One of the male officers led Ryan away down a corridor to the left. Another pulled Louie through a series of doors and then through a corridor that ended at a small room with dark green walls and floor. A long, white polymer table that was covered with plastifilm stood in the center and matching cabinets lined one wall.

The officer, a burly man with a gold stud in his left ear, disabled the electrocuffs. "Take off all your clothes."

Louie cringed.

"Now! When the technician gets here, she's not gonna want to wait around for you to get undressed."

With trembling fingers, Louie stripped, hanging shirt, shorts, and underwear from the hook on the back of the door. A moment later, a woman wearing a white smock over a dark green citysuit entered the room. "Lie down on the table. We need to see what you've been up to."

Even through the plastifilm, the polymer table felt warm against Louie's bare skin. With legs spread, knees pointing at opposite walls, Louie endured the technician's probing. The woman handed the patrol officer a tray containing several swabs and a small glass vial. "Here's your evidence. Now let the poor thing get dressed."

The next morning, Louie sat upright at a square table, facing Meg's and Greta's glowers across the polymer tabletop. The windowless walls of the detention center's visiting room amplified the chatter of myriad conversations. Family members were gathered at a dozen tables, facing arrestees who wore bright orange shorts and sleeveless tops.

Meg and Greta, their eyes red from weeping, clasped their hands together in white-knuckled tightness on the table. Both women wore tailored citysuits in coordinated colors. Around their necks hung medallions engraved with the other's name and the date of their first partnering twenty-four years ago.

Meg, her short grey hair rumpled as if she had just gotten out of bed, spoke first. "Louie, how could you? Now, you'll never get accepted to a conservatory. All that musical talent, all your hours of practice, wasted."

Greta shook her head, the creases around her green eyes deepening, her luxurious auburn hair pulled back into a stern ponytail. "Why, Louise? How could you have sex with a boy? What were you thinking?" Of everyone Louie knew, only Greta refused to use her preferred nickname.

"We're in love." Louie folded her hands in her lap and stared at them. The polymer chair seat was sticky against her bare legs. "We want to partner when we graduate."

Greta and Meg gasped in unison, and Louie looked up to see her mothers staring at her, open mouthed. Meg's blue eyes filled with tears and she collapsed into Greta's arms. Greta held Meg close. Louie returned her gaze to her hands. When had three of her fingernails broken off?

"We'll get a good attorney, Meg." Greta stroked her partner's hair. "My boss knows people."

"How could she do this to us?" Meg sobbed into Greta's shoulder. "Why couldn't she be a normal teen?"

Louie looked up to see Greta glaring at her over Meg's head, a grimace playing across her thin lips. "Louise, you know you won't ever see that boy again, except maybe in court. Please don't talk with anyone about partnering with him. It won't help your case."

The thought of never again holding Ryan,

never knowing the touch of his skin against hers, never kissing him, triggered the tears Louie had suppressed since arriving at the detention center. She covered her face with her hands, her shoulders shaking with sobs. Greta released Meg, and both women reached across the table. They ran their hands up and down Louie's arms.

"No touching the arrestees," a voice crackled from the receiver in the center of the table. Greta and Meg pulled back with a start. Louie longed to curl up like a child in one of their laps and rest her head on Meg's plump bosom or Greta's almost-flat chest. But, the voice informed them that time was up and all visitors had to vacate the premises immediately. Weeping silently, Louie watched Greta and Meg walk from the room, Greta's arm draped over Meg's shoulder.

During the trial, Louise sat on a chair in a narrow hearing room, the dark green walls bare except for the array of vidscreens and a camera pointed at her face. She saw Ryan for the first time since their arrest, but only on one of the screens. On a second screen, she could watch the judge, who wore green vestments and a matching biretta and sat behind a raised brown polymer desk at one end of a courtroom. The third screen showed Louie's attorney and the prosecutor. The six monitors showing the jurors'

faces were tiled together on a fourth screen.

Ryan also witnessed the proceedings from the confines of a narrow room, alone with screens and camera. He sat with shoulders hunched over and his chin on his chest. He looked haggard with dark circles under his eyes. She wondered if he'd suffered as much abuse at the hands of his fellow arrestees as she had. During three months in detention, the others had harassed, beaten, and taunted her. They painted a black "P" for pervert on her forehead and one time three held her down while another molested her with a broken energy wand.

"We received an anonymous tip that Louise Decker and Ryan Bister were involved in an illegal relationship." Louie looked at the previously dark fifth screen and recognized the arresting officer as the one who had witnessed her exam. "On the twenty-second day of the third month, we followed the two to a vacant dwell in a structure managed by one of Bister's fathers. Because he does maintenance for his father, Bister has voice access to the structure and the dwells in it. We waited outside the dwell and arrested them when they emerged."

The officer wrinkled his nose, although his voice remained neutral. "When Decker was examined by medical personnel, they found fluid composed of Bister's DNA in her vagina." Louie heard muttering from spectators, although she couldn't see them on any monitors.

"Quiet!" The judge struck the bell that sat on

her desk with a small metal hammer. "If you people can't maintain decorum, I'll empty the court."

The prosecutor handed the judge specimens collected during Louie's medical exam, along with her and Ryan's genetic identifiers. Neither Louie's nor Ryan's defense attorneys, who had not asked the officer any questions, presented opposing testimony or evidence. The prosecution's brief summation warned the jury to make an example of them or they'd see hordes of other young people experimenting with heterosexuality.

When the prosecutor took his seat, the young woman representing Louie stood and adjusted her grey smock. She turned and faced the six monitors in the courtroom that displayed the faces of the jurors.

"Citizens of the City, you need to remember that only a few hundred years ago, society treated homosexuals as outcasts."

Several members of the jury sneered.

"Laws forbade what they called sodomy, even in the privacy of one's own home, and laws prohibited homosexual couples from partnering. "

The sneers turned to wide-eyed disbelief.

"Until technology allowed us to take procreation out of the bedroom, men and women were required to have sex with each other in order to produce the next generation."

Louie heard gasps from off-camera. The judge picked up the hammer, but the room quieted and she set it down.

The prosecutor stood. "Your Grace, I object

to this discourse. History has no bearing on this case, only current law."

"Please indulge me, your Grace," the defense attorney said. "We haven't disputed the facts. My summation speaks to consequences, which is the only area that we can address."

The judge frowned. "I'll give you some leeway, Attorney Reiser. But don't take too much of the court's time."

The attorney turned back to the jury. "Those who take the time to study some of the ancient books preserved in museums can learn that for millennia human beings mated with the opposite sex just like the animals that once ran wild across the planet. We have tried to condition those instincts out of our youth through education and opportunity. But, members of the jury, we cannot completely mute the biological urges that governed our behavior for thousands upon thousands of years." The attorney had assured Meg and Greta that she would mount an unusual defense, but Louie had *no* idea where the woman got her information. The judge stared at the attorney, ignoring the hammer resting by her hand and the muttering from spectators.

"Should Louise and Ryan have violated the law by making love with each other? No. Should they be punished for falling in love and seeking a physical manifestation of that love? No, not in a society that encourages young people to enjoy sexual relationships once they reach puberty.

"I would ask your Grace to take human biological history, raging hormones, and the impetuousness of youth into consideration in deciding the fate of these two young people on the verge of adulthood. Give them the opportunity to redeem themselves rather than destroying their future for a foolish indiscretion."

The attorney took her seat and Louie watched the faces of the jurors. She saw disgust and loathing in their expressions. Nowhere did she see a sympathetic smile or a compassionate nod. A tear drifted down her cheek.

After less than an hour, the judge returned to the courtroom and the jurors' monitors were turned back on. Louie watched Ryan's eyes dart from screen to screen. She longed to see him in person, to touch his face, to hold his hand.

The jury read its statement in unison. "On this twentieth day of the sixth month of the one hundred and seventy-sixth year of the fourth era, we the people of the City of VanSeaPort find both defendants, Louise Decker and Ryan Bister, guilty of fornicating with the opposite sex in violation of the Morality Code. We also recommend that the maximum sentence be imposed."

The judge nodded toward the jury. "The Court thanks you for your service." She folded her hands together on her desk, and looked directly at the camera transmitting her image to the screens in the two hearing rooms. "Whatever the history of human sexuality, in this City the law today prohibits intercourse between men and women. Based on defense testimony, I can only guess that these laws were developed to protect society from the fertility consequences of such activities. You have knowingly and flagrantly broken these laws. Therefore, I sentence each of you to serve ten years in City detention."

Louie dropped her face to her hands and bent over her knees, weeping.

"However...because you are both young and this is your first offense, I will commute your sentences provided you meet certain conditions. First, you will both serve monitored probation for the entire ten years. Second, during your probation, neither of you will have any contact with the other. Third, you will each perform five hundred hours of penance service to the City for every year of your probation. Finally, you will actively participate in intimacy counseling, and your counselors will report on your progress to the court.

"If you fail to meet any one of these conditions, you will serve the entire ten years of your sentence in City detention, no matter how long you have been on probation. Do you understand these conditions?"

Louie shook her head, but her attorney, and Ryan's, answered "Yes, your Grace."

The judge tapped the bell, rose, and walked from the courtroom. A guard unlocked the hearing room door and escorted Louie back to her cell.

For the fourth morning in a row, Louie's roiling stomach woke her. She ran out of her bedroom to the hygiene closet and spent half an hour bent over the toilet. When she emerged, her face pale and her eyes red, she found Meg waiting.

"Do I need to take you to the medfac? You don't eat much and it seems you're sick every morning."

"I'll be fine. I just miss Ryan."

"You've got to stop talking like that, Louie. I hope you don't mention his name to your intimacy counselor?"

Louie shook her head, too queasy to argue.

"You need to move on with your life. I've talked to my boss. I told her you've got some talent for design, and she's willing to give you part-time work. I know it's not music, but no one's gonna to hire a synthharpist who doesn't have certification."

Louie nodded. She had nothing better to do in between counseling sessions and the ten hours she spent each week cleaning hydro tanks from the building's roof garden than to obsessively search historybases for records on heterosexuality. Following references to food riots in the middle of the twenty-first century, she found discussions about improvements in laboratory reproduction methods and genetic screening, but nothing about men and women having sex to procreate.

Louie walked home from her job working at Meg's office rather than take the monorail to minimize the time she had to spend under her mothers' worried glares. Her route took her past the Bibliomuseum and one afternoon she ventured inside. The first room she entered took her breath away. As big as the entire office where sixty people worked, its ceilings rose higher than Louie could see without tilting her head back. A single desk, made of some kind of brown polymer that gleamed in a way she had never seen before, stood near the doorway. Behind it, twenty tables, each surrounded by four or five chairs, spread out across a floor made of another unfamiliar type of polymer.

A woman who looked old enough to be her mothers' grandmother sat behind the desk. "Hi, this your first time?" She handed Louie a glossy, flat item. "Please read this. It's an introduction to our museum."

Louie tried to swipe the screen, but the letters remained static. The item said it was a "brochure" created by printing ink on paper as, apparently, were most of the texts in the museum. It identified the material of the desk and tables as "wood," and the floor as "marble."

Louie read the definitions, explanations, and rules, shook her head, and returned it to the woman behind the desk.

"Enjoy your visit. Feel free to stop back here if you have any questions."

"Thanks." Louie wandered between the tables to the curved wall, which was lined with shelves reaching to the ceiling. Rows of antiques crowded each shelf. Louie ran her hand along the "spines" of the "books," bound between hardened fabric or glossy covers. Following the shelf until she reached a doorway, she peered out to see a long dim corridor that was lined on both sides with rows of "books."

For the next few weeks, Louie spent her after-shift hours extracting volumes from the shelves and reading by the light of "lamps" centered on each table. She learned the numerical filing system, how to push the ladder across the shelves to reach higher books, and how to search through the "catalog" with its small, square pieces of paper that filled drawer after drawer in the large wooden cabinet that lined one of the Bibliomuseum's many corridors.

In the fiction sections, she found classic stories that she remembered reading in school. But, although they seemed familiar, she discovered one major difference in all the romances. *Romeo and Julian* from school became *Romeo and Juliet* on paper. Rhett Butler not Rita had loved Scarlett O'Hara in *Gone with the Wind*, and the partner rescued by Liam Rollin in *City of Love* was Theresa not Terry Jaroset.

Further exploration of the museum yielded ancient textbooks that included information on human reproduction and psychology. "Magazines" printed on yellowed pages contained articles that discussed homosexuality as a disease.

Shown how to scroll through "newspaper" articles on a lighted box, she read debates about Earth running out of resources, essays on the need for population control, and stories of "queers" persecuted for homosexual relationships.

At home, Louie spent most of her time connected, her synthharp sitting untouched in the corner. Something the judge said nagged at Louie, and she looked up the trial transcript. The comment that "..in this City the law today...," sent Louie off on another search through the historybases. She found references to people who lived outside the Cities, who grew fruits and vegetables in dirt, who ate animals. After weeks of research, Louie found a link to communicate with "FT," a man who said he knew people from the Independent Alaskan Republic.

She explained her situation, coyly at first. But he recognized her case from the few details she shared. Rather than condemning her, much to her delight, he promised help.

Because Louie still spent fifteen minutes spewing the contents of her stomach into the toilet each morning, Meg dragged her to their sector medfac. Louie watched dozens of people -- some bleeding, others pale and sweaty with fever, a few reeking of synthol abuse -- get called from the crowded triage room.

Finally, a young woman ushered them into a

tiny room that was crowded with two chairs, a polymer table covered in plastifilm, and a locked cabinet. A poster reminding patients to update their STvacs provided the only color relief to the unbroken beige of floor and walls. When the NP examining Louie found nothing amiss, she unlocked the cabinet, pulled out patches attached to wires and stuck them all over Louie's skin. After staring at the screen for five minutes, she gave Louie a vial, took her to a hygiene closet, and told her to urinate into the vial. Another woman in a white smock came in and pricked her arm to draw blood. By then, Louie was trembling so much the woman had to ask Meg to hold Louie's arm still. Ten minutes later another technician made Louie spread her legs so she could swab a sample of her secretions.

When they allowed Louie to put her clothes back, she waited with Meg for forty-five minutes, both staring at the wall in silence. Meg had ignored Louie's plea to *just walk out* for the fifth time, when a hunched over man with only a few strands of white hair clinging to his scalp, wobbled into the room. Meg stood so that he could sit in her chair.

He peered at Louie through watery eyes. "You're that little pervert convicted of fornicating with a male, aren't ya?" His voice sounded creaky and he smelled like stale bread.

Meg responded. "I don't know what that has to do with the fact that my daughter suffers from nausea and listlessness."

"Oh, it has everything to do with it. Your daughter's pregnant."

"What does that mean?"

The doctor pointed at Louie's belly. "She has a child growing in there."

"I don't understand?"

The doctor shoved his hands in the pocket of his smock and straightened his shoulders. "Before we perfected incubators, babies gestated inside women's uteri. Of course, we fertilized the eggs in the laboratory and then implanted them, so we could genetically select for optimum results. But sometimes foetal problems developed because pregnant women were exposed to adverse environmental factors."

Meg stared at the doctor, mouth open, eyes wide.

"Centuries before *I* began practicing medicine, we didn't even have the technology for in vitro fertilization. A man impregnated a woman by inserting his penis in her vagina and ejaculating his sperm." The doctor grimaced and shuddered.

Louie remembered the wonder of the moment when Ryan gave himself to her completely for the first time. Her eyes filled with tears and a whimper escaped her lips.

"Don't worry, child." The doctor patted Louie on the shoulder. "I'm something of a student of ancient medical practices. That's why I've been brought in. I've done some research on a procedure that will remove the foetus with no lasting ill effects."

"Can I keep the baby?" Louie blurted out. At the Bibliomuseum, she had found information about women who gave birth and nursed their babies, generating formula in their breasts. The idea had seemed strange, but now she found it comforting.

"Well, no. The foetus isn't viable and it can't be transferred to an incubator at this stage of development." Again, the doctor patted Louie's shoulder. She recoiled from his touch. "It's for the best, child. You don't know what kind of problems random genetics might cause this baby. Children used to suffer all kinds of birth defects and illnesses. Why, in ancient times, more than half of all children born to women didn't survive to adulthood."

"No!" Louie screamed. She ran from the room and elbowed her way through the crowd waiting in triage out into the street.

Without pausing to think, she tore up the conveyor to the monorail and boarded the train that she had ridden so many times with Ryan. A stranger crowded next to her, standing unusually close despite the almost empty aisle.

"Don't turn around to look at me, but I know who you are and, as promised, I've come to help you," he whispered in her ear.

Louie closed her eyes, her throat growing tight, her palms slippery on the strap above her head.

"I'm FT, the IAR liaison you contacted. I've been following you, looking for an opportunity to approach you when your mothers weren't around."

Despite his warning, Louie snapped her head around to look at the man. Soft brown eyes peered down at her from a weathered, bearded face framed by shoulder-length grey hair. The man wore a faded blue citysuit and carried a worn nylon bag slung over his shoulder. He shook his head, and Louie turned to stare at the comvid screen showing ads pushing hallucinogens.

"We need to go somewhere we can talk without being seen, Msr. Decker," he said.

Louie knew she couldn't go back to her dwell. Her parents would insist she kill the baby growing inside her--Ryan's baby. If they could escape the City and find the IAR, maybe they could live together. Louie whispered Ryan's name into the transmitter implanted in her left wrist, grateful she never deleted his contact code. Hours seemed to pass before he answered.

"Louie, why are you calling?" Ryan's voice whispered in her ear.

"I've got to talk to you. It's important."

"More important than the ten years we'll spend in detention because of this conversation?"

"Yes."

"Where are you?"

Louie looked at the computer display over

the door. "Near the 356th Street monorail exit."

"Go to 437th and 745th Avenue. The green structure on the corner. Dwell sixty-two."

She repeated the information to FT, who was looking around the car at the other passengers reading news bits on the display, watching the comvid, or lost in their own VR headsets. He reached into his bag and pulled out a small device. When he waved it over Louie's wrist, her electromonitor fell off onto his waiting palm. After another furtive glance around the car, he attached it to the strap next to the one Louie clung to.

When they reached the stop, Louie scanned the car and darted out just before the doors shushed closed and the train pulled away in a hiss of hydraulics. She didn't see any green Morality Patrol uniforms, so she tore down the conveyor, paused at the bottom to get her bearings, then scampered through the streets to the structure Ryan had described. FT followed at a leisurely pace, but with his long legs he was still in sight every time she glanced back.

Louie called Ryan again from the lobby. When the security doors opened, she and FT ducked through and entered the waiting lift on the other side of the lobby, riding it up to the sixth floor. FT stayed by the lift until Ryan opened the door to the vacant dwell across the corridor, then he dashed inside with them.

"He can help us, Ryan," Louie said. She held up her naked wrist. "He took off my monitor."

Ryan looked skeptical, but he closed the door. Louie threw herself into his arms and clung to him, sobbing and gasping for breath. "I don't want to live without you, Ryan. I love you, I want to partner with you, and I'm pregerant!"

Ryan peeled Louie's hands from around his neck. His fingers gripped her shoulders, keeping her at arm's length. "You're what?"

"I believe she means pregnant. Congratulations."

Ryan scowled at FT. He looked worn out and had lost several kilos. Instead of his usual retro jeans and shirt, Ryan wore a conventional city-suit in mauve lyester that was speckled with orange paint.

"Msr. Bister, I'm Forrest Terrel from the IAR."

Ryan stared at him, his head cocked to one side.

"Don't they teach you anything in City schools? IAR, Independent Alaskan Republic." Terrel gave him a sympathetic smile. "Do you know what pregnant means, Ryan?"

Ryan shook his head.

"Louise is carrying your baby."

Ryan's brows drew together, he pressed his lips into a thin line, and looked at Louie. "I don't understand."

"Remember what Louise's attorney said about the way the ancients mated?"

Although he nodded, Ryan's expression didn't change.

"When you had sex with Louise, you deposited your sperm. As a result, one of her eggs was fertilized and she now has a baby, your baby, growing inside her uterus."

Ryan's eyes opened wider and his jaw dropped. He clapped his hand over his mouth, his skin took on a greenish tinge, and he sucked in air through his nose.

Tears spilled down Louie's cheeks. She had grown up knowing the competition to earn parenting rights prevented many couples from having children. Now she had Ryan's baby growing inside her. She didn't want to give it up. But watching Ryan, she realized she had mistakenly assumed he would react the same way she had to the news and would want the same things she did.

Terrel put one hand on Ryan's shoulder. "I know the news comes as a bit of a shock, son. But the ancients expected a man to take responsibility for the children he spawned, and so do we. The IAR broke away from the Union of North America because we couldn't accept the Morality and Identity Laws, among others. In the Republic, we try to follow, as much as possible, the old ways. We don't use hovers or cells there." He picked up Louie's hand and examined the small button of her transmitter under the skin on the back of her wrist. "Or monorails or even connections. We raise animals and grow plants for our food."

Releasing Louie's hand, Terrel paced back and forth in the empty dwell, staying close to the wall opposite the window. "We have other liaisons like myself here in the City. We learn to use the technology so that we can help people like you and Ryan escape. Unfortunately, you're facing a difficult and dangerous journey. And, when you get to Alaska, you'll have a lot of catching up to do. Most of what you've been taught about how to get along won't apply there."

He stopped with his back to the wall and stared at Louie. "As to your situation, the IAR doesn't control the population through artificial procreation. Men and women partner and have babies without incubators or petri dishes. After a couple produces two children, they avoid additional pregnancies by using medication or barriers."

"Two children?" Louie blinked away her tears. "Couples are allowed two children?"

"Yes." The man smiled at Louie. "Because our population isn't dense, our goal is to maintain, not reduce, our numbers."

"But, but, what about morality patrols?" Louie shivered.

"We don't have morality patrols in the IAR."

Ryan took both of Louie's hands in his and stared into her eyes. His skin had returned to its normal sandy hue, and the warmth of his palms against hers gave her strength. "Look, Louie, this is ..." He squeezed her hands. "I know it won't be easy. We have to sneak out of the City and we could get caught. That means ten years of detention. But I want to live with you too, and we can't do that here."

"In the IAR, we could be together?" Louie asked Terrel. She and Ryan had shared a fantasy of living as partners--talked about sleeping in the same bed, waking up together, raising a child--even though they knew that only same-gender couples had those options.

Terrel smiled. "You would have to get married, but you could be together."

"Married?"

"When a couple wishes to partner, they participate in a ceremony. During the ceremony, they promise to stay true to each other and take responsibility for their children."

Louie stared at Terrel. "We could keep the baby?"

"Of course, child."

"When can we leave?"

"Usually, I would suggest waiting a few days so I could reach out to others to help you along your route. But the Morality Patrol will discover you two had contact when they review the electromonitor data. We need to get you away from here before they arrest you for violating probation."

Louie thought of her bedroom at home, her clothing, synthharp, collectibles. "I should send word to my moms."

Terrel looked at Ryan.

"I should send word, too." He grinned, the smile lighting up his dark eyes. "But there's nothing to stop me from leaving *right now*."

Looking up and down Louie's slender form, emphasized by the tight shorts and shirt, Terrel pulled on his light grey beard. "We need to put you in some clothes that'll disguise your figure. Two men traveling together will attract less attention than a man and a woman. Do you have credits?"

She and Ryan nodded. His father paid him well for maintenance work, and Louie had credits now too, from her job at Meg's office.

"After we buy Louise some appropriate apparel, we can find a public connection so you two can send messages to your parents. Louise, go on ahead and find yourself something like this." Terrel pulled at the loose fabric of his citysuit. "Make sure it's a little big rather than tight. Ryan and I will meet you ...?" He looked at Ryan.

"Lester's. It's three blocks away on 745th."

Terrel removed Ryan's electromonitor and set it next to the cooking unit in the kitchen. He pulled another electronic device from his bag and pressed it against Ryan's wrist. Ryan winced and when Terrel released him shook his hand for several seconds.

"That was the easy part." Terrel put the device up to Ryan's ear. "Brace yourself."

Ryan leaned against the wall. When Terrel stepped back, Ryan's face was pale and sweat covered his brow. Slowly he slid down the wall until he landed with a thud on his rear.

Terrel held out a hand to Louie and she placed the palm of her left hand on his. She felt the zap that fried her transmitter and bit her lip to avoid crying out in pain. The burn only lasted for a few seconds. Without prompting, she leaned against the wall next to where Ryan still sat on the orange carpet. Excruciating agony shot through her head and she collapsed. When her eyes fluttered open, Ryan held her in his arms.

Terrel crouched next to them, his fingers against her pulse. "Sorry you had to endure that. When you make it to the IAR, you can have those surgically removed. But, at least now they can't be used to track you."

Louie pushed herself to her feet, holding onto the wall until she felt steady enough to walk. Ryan stood up as well and she looked up into his worried eyes, "I'm okay. Let's go."

He nodded.

Louie smiled for the first time since her arrest.

𝕷